SMITH
OF
WOOTTON MAJOR

J. R. R. TOLKIEN

SMITH
OF
WOOTTON MAJOR

WITH ILLUSTRATIONS BY
PAULINE BAYNES

HOUGHTON MIFFLIN COMPANY BOSTON

1978

SMITH
OF
WOOTTON MAJOR

SMITH
OF
WOOTTON MAJOR

HERE was a village once, not very long ago for those with long memories, nor very far away for those with long legs. Wootton Major it was called because it was larger than Wootton Minor, a few miles away deep in the trees; but it was not very large, though it was at that time prosperous, and a fair number of folk lived in it, good, bad, and mixed, as is usual.

It was a remarkable village in its way, being well known in the country round about for the skill of its workers in various crafts, but most of all for its cooking. It had a large Kitchen which belonged to the Village Council, and the Master Cook was an important person. The Cook's House and the Kitchen adjoined the Great Hall, the largest and oldest building in the place and the most beautiful. It was built of good stone and good oak and was well tended, though it was no longer painted or gilded as it had been once upon a time. In the Hall the villagers held their meetings and debates, and their public feasts, and their family gatherings. So the Cook was kept busy, since for all these occasions he had to provide suitable fare. For the festivals, of which there were many in the course of a year, the fare that was thought suitable was plentiful and rich.

There was one festival to which all looked forward, for it was the only one held in winter. It went on for a week, and on its last day at sundown there was a merrymaking called The Feast of Good Children, to which not many were invited. No doubt some who deserved to be asked were overlooked, and some who did not were invited by mistake; for that is the way of things, however careful those who arrange such matters may try to be. In any case it was largely by chance of birthday that any child came in for the Twenty-four Feast, since that was only held once in twenty-four years, and only twenty-four children were invited. For that occasion the Master Cook was expected to do his best, and in addition to many other good things it was the custom for him to make the Great Cake. By the excellence (or otherwise) of this his name was chiefly remembered, for a Master Cook seldom if ever lasted long enough in office to make a second Great Cake.

There came a time, however, when the reigning Master Cook, to everyone's surprise, since it had never happened before, suddenly announced that he needed a holiday; and he went away, no one knew where; and when he came back some months later he seemed rather changed. He had been a kind man who liked to see other people enjoying themselves, but he was himself serious, and said very little. Now he was merrier, and often said and did most laughable things; and at feasts he would himself sing gay songs, which was not expected of Master Cooks. Also he brought back with him an Apprentice; and that astonished the Village.

It was not astonishing for the Master Cook to have an apprentice. It was usual. The Master chose one in due time, and he taught him all that he could; and as they both grew older the apprentice took on more of the important work, so that when the Master retired or died there he was, ready to take over the office and become Master Cook in his turn. But this Master had never chosen an apprentice. He had always said 'time enough yet', or 'I'm keeping my eyes open and I'll choose one when I find one to suit me'. But now he brought with him a mere boy, and not one from the village. He was more lithe than the Wootton lads and quicker, soft-spoken and very polite, but ridiculously young for the work, barely in his teens by the look of him. Still, choosing his apprentice was the Master Cook's affair, and no one had the right to interfere in it; so the boy remained and stayed in the Cook's House until he was old enough to find lodgings for himself. People soon became used to seeing him about, and he made a few friends. They and the Cook called him Alf, but to the rest he was just Prentice.

The next surprise came only three years later. One spring morning the Master Cook took off his tall white hat, folded up his clean aprons, hung up his white coat, took a stout ash stick and a small bag, and departed. He said goodbye to the apprentice. No one else was about.

'Goodbye for now, Alf', he said. 'I leave you to manage things as best you can, which is always very well. I expect it will turn out all right. If we meet again, I hope to hear all about it. Tell them that I've gone on another holiday, but this time I shan't be coming back again'.

There was quite a stir in the village when Prentice gave this message to people who came to the Kitchen. 'What a thing to do!' they said. 'And without warning or farewell! What are we going to do without any Master Cook? He has left no one to take his place'. In all their discussions no one ever thought of making young Prentice into Cook. He had grown a bit taller but still looked like a boy, and he had only served for three years.

In the end for lack of anyone better they appointed a man of the village, who could cook well enough in a small way. When he was younger he had helped the Master at busy times, but the Master had never taken to him and would not have him as apprentice. He was now a solid sort of man with a wife and children, and careful with money. 'At any rate he won't go off without notice', they said, 'and poor cooking is better than none. It is seven years till the next Great Cake, and by that time he should be able to manage it'.

Nokes, for that was his name, was very pleased with the turn things had taken. He had always wished to become Master Cook, and had never doubted that he could manage it. For some time, when he was alone in the Kitchen, he used to put on the tall white hat and look at himself in a polished frying pan and say: 'How do you do, Master. That hat suits you properly, might have been made for you. I hope things go well with you'.

Things went well enough; for at first Nokes did his best, and he had Prentice to help him. Indeed he learned a lot from him by watching him slyly, though that Nokes never admitted. But in due course the time for the Twenty-four Feast drew near, and Nokes had to think about making the Great Cake. Secretly he was worried about it, for although with seven years' practice he could turn out passable cakes and pastries for ordinary occasions, he knew that his Great Cake would be eagerly awaited, and would have to satisfy severe critics. Not only the children. A smaller cake of the same materials and baking had to be provided for those who came to help at the feast. Also it was expected that the Great Cake should have something novel and surprising about it and not be a mere repetition of the one before.

His chief notion was that it should be very sweet and rich; and he decided that it should be entirely covered in sugar-icing (at which Prentice had a clever hand). 'That will make it pretty and fairylike', he thought. Fairies and sweets were two of the very few notions he had about the tastes of children. Fairies he thought one grew out of; but of sweets he remained very fond. 'Ah! fairylike', he said, 'that gives me an idea'; and so it came into his head that he would stick a little doll on a pinnacle in the middle of the Cake, dressed all in white, with a little wand in her hand ending in a tinsel star, and *Fairy Queen* written in pink icing round her feet.

But when he began preparing the materials for the cake-making he found that he had only dim memories of what should go *inside* a Great Cake; so he looked in some old books of recipes left behind by previous cooks. They puzzled him, even when he could make out their handwriting, for they mentioned many things that he had not heard of, and some that he had forgotten and now had no time to get; but he thought he might try one or two of the spices that the books spoke of. He scratched his head and remembered an old black box with several different compartments in which the last Cook had once kept spices and other things for special cakes. He had not looked at it since he took over, but after a search he found it on a high shelf in the store-room.

He took it down and blew the dust off the lid; but when he opened it he found that very little of the spices was left, and they were dry and musty. But in one compartment in the corner he discovered a small star, hardly as big as one of our sixpences, black-looking as if it was made of silver but was tarnished. 'That's funny!' he said as he held it up to the light.

'No, it isn't!' said a voice behind him, so suddenly that he jumped. It was the voice of Prentice, and he had never spoken to the Master in that tone before. Indeed he seldom spoke to Nokes at all unless he was spoken to first. Very right and proper in a youngster; he might be clever with icing but he had a lot to learn yet: that was Nokes's opinion.

'What do you mean, young fellow?' he said, not much pleased. 'If it isn't funny what is it?'

'It is *fay*', said Prentice. 'It comes from Faery'.

Then the Cook laughed. 'All right, all right', he said. 'It means much the same; but call it that if you like. You'll grow up some day. Now you can get on with stoning the raisins. If you notice any funny fairy ones, tell me'.

'What are you going to do with the star, Master?' said Prentice.

'Put it into the Cake, of course', said the Cook. 'Just the thing, especially if it's *fairy*', he sniggered. 'I daresay you've been to children's parties yourself, and not so long ago either, where little trinkets like this were stirred into the mixture, and little coins and what not. Anyway we do that in this village: it amuses the children'.

'But this isn't a trinket, Master, it's a fay-star', said Prentice.

'So you've said already', snapped the Cook. 'Very

well, I'll tell the children. It'll make them laugh'.

'I don't think it will, Master', said Prentice. 'But it's the right thing to do, quite right'.

'Who do you think you're talking to?' said Nokes.

In time the Cake was made and baked and iced, mostly by Prentice. 'As you are so set on fairies, I'll let you make the Fairy Queen', Nokes said to him.

'Very good, Master', he answered. 'I'll do it if you are too busy. But it was your idea and not mine'.

'It's my place to have ideas, and not yours', said Nokes.

At the Feast the Cake stood in the middle of the long table, inside a ring of twenty-four red candles. Its top rose into a small white mountain, up the sides of which grew little trees glittering as if with frost; on its summit stood a tiny white figure on one foot like a snow-maiden dancing, and in her hand was a minute wand of ice sparkling with light.

The children looked at it with wide eyes, and one or two clapped their hands, crying: 'Isn't it pretty and fairylike!' That delighted the Cook, but the apprentice looked displeased. They were both present: the Master to cut up the Cake when the time came, and the apprentice to sharpen the knife and hand it to him.

At last the Cook took the knife and stepped up to the table. 'I should tell you, my dears', he said, 'that inside this lovely icing there is a cake made of many nice things to eat; but also stirred well in there are many pretty little things, trinkets and little coins and

what not, and I'm told that it is lucky to find one in your slice. There are twenty-four in the Cake, so there should be one for each of you, if the Fairy Queen plays fair. But she doesn't always do so: she's a tricky little creature. You ask Mr. Prentice'. The apprentice turned away and studied the faces of the children.

'No! I'm forgetting', said the Cook. 'There's twenty-five this evening. There's also a little silver star, a special magic one, or so Mr. Prentice says. So be careful! If you break one of your pretty front teeth on it, the magic star won't mend it. But I expect it's a specially lucky thing to find, all the same'.

It was a good cake, and no one had any fault to find with it, except that it was no bigger than was needed. When it was all cut up there was a large slice for each of the children, but nothing left over: no coming again. The slices soon disappeared, and every now and then a trinket or a coin was discovered. Some found one, and some found two, and several found none; for that is the way luck goes, whether there is a doll with a wand on the cake or not. But when the Cake was all eaten, there was no sign of any magic star.

'Bless me!' said the Cook. 'Then it can't have been made of silver after all; it must have melted. Or perhaps Mr. Prentice was right and it was really magical, and it's just vanished and gone back to Fairyland. Not a nice trick to play, I don't think'. He looked at Prentice with a smirk, and Prentice looked at him with dark eyes and did not smile at all.

All the same, the silver star was indeed a fay-star: the apprentice was not one to make mistakes about things of that sort. What had happened was that one of the boys at the Feast had swallowed it without ever noticing it, although he had found a silver coin in his slice and had given it to Nell, the little girl next to him: she looked so disappointed at finding nothing lucky in hers. He sometimes wondered what had really become of the star, and did not know that it had remained with him, tucked away in some place where it could not be felt; for that was what it was intended to do. There it waited for a long time, until its day came.

The Feast had been in mid-winter, but it was now June, and the night was hardly dark at all. The boy got up before dawn, for he did not wish to sleep: it was his tenth birthday. He looked out of the window, and the world seemed quiet and expectant. A little breeze, cool and fragrant, stirred the waking trees. Then the dawn came, and far away he heard the dawn-song of the birds beginning, growing as it came towards him, until it rushed over him, filling all the land round the house, and passed on like a wave of music into the West, as the sun rose above the rim of the world.

'It reminds me of Faery', he heard himself say; 'but in Faery the people sing too'. Then he began to sing, high and clear, in strange words that he seemed to

know by heart; and in that moment the star fell out of his mouth and he caught it on his open hand. It was bright silver now, glistening in the sunlight; but it quivered and rose a little, as if it was about to fly away. Without thinking he clapped his hand to his head, and there the star stayed in the middle of his forehead, and he wore it for many years.

Few people in the village noticed it though it was not invisible to attentive eyes; but it became part of his face, and it did not usually shine at all. Some of its light passed into his eyes; and his voice, which had begun to grow beautiful as soon as the star came to him, became ever more beautiful as he grew up. People liked to hear him speak, even if it was no more than a 'good morning'.

He became well known in his country, not only in his own village but in many others round about, for his good workmanship. His father was a smith, and he followed him in his craft and bettered it. Smithson he was called while his father was still alive, and then just Smith. For by that time he was the best smith between Far Easton and the Westwood, and he could make all kinds of things of iron in his smithy. Most of them, of course, were plain and useful, meant for daily needs: farm tools, carpenters' tools, kitchen tools and pots and pans, bars and bolts and hinges, pot-hooks, fire-dogs, and horse-shoes, and the like. They were strong and lasting, but they also had a grace about them, being shapely in their kinds, good to handle and to look at.

23

But some things, when he had time, he made for delight; and they were beautiful, for he could work iron into wonderful forms that looked as light and delicate as a spray of leaves and blossom, but kept the stern strength of iron, or seemed even stronger. Few could pass by one of the gates or lattices that he made without stopping to admire it; no one could pass through it once it was shut. He sang when he was making things of this sort; and when Smith began to sing those nearby stopped their own work and came to the smithy to listen.

That was all that most people knew about him. It was enough indeed and more than most men and women in the village achieved, even those who were skilled and hard-working. But there was more to know. For Smith became acquainted with Faery, and some regions of it he knew as well as any mortal can; though since too many had become like Nokes, he spoke of this to few people, except his wife and his children. His wife was Nell, to whom he gave the silver coin, and his daughter was Nan, and his son was Ned Smithson. From them it could not have been kept secret anyway, for they sometimes saw the star shining on his forehead, when he came back from one of the long walks he would take alone now and then in the evening, or when he returned from a journey.

From time to time he would go off, sometimes

walking, sometimes riding, and it was generally supposed that it was on business; and sometimes it was, and sometimes it was not. At any rate not to get orders for work, or to buy pig-iron and charcoal and other supplies, though he attended to such things with care and knew how to turn an honest penny into twopence, as the saying went. But he had business of its own kind in Faery, and he was welcome there; for the star shone bright on his brow, and he was as safe as a mortal can be in that perilous country. The Lesser Evils avoided the star, and from the Greater Evils he was guarded.

For that he was grateful, for he soon became wise and understood that the marvels of Faery cannot be approached without danger, and that many of the Evils cannot be challenged without weapons of power too great for any mortal to wield. He remained a learner and explorer, not a warrior; and though in time he could have forged weapons that in his own world would have had power enough to become the matter of great tales and be worth a king's ransom, he knew that in Faery they would have been of small account. So among all the things that he made it is not remembered that he ever forged a sword or a spear or an arrow-head.

In Faery at first he walked for the most part quietly among the lesser folk and the gentler creatures in the woods and meads of fair valleys, and by the bright waters in which at night strange stars shone and at dawn the gleaming peaks of far mountains were mirrored. Some of his briefer visits he spent looking only at one tree or one flower; but later in longer journeys he had seen things of both beauty and terror that he could not clearly remember nor report to his friends, though he knew that they dwelt deep in his heart. But some things he did not forget, and they remained in his mind as wonders and mysteries that he often recalled.

When he first began to walk far without a guide he thought he would discover the further bounds of the land; but great mountains rose before him, and going by long ways round about them he came at last to a desolate shore. He stood beside the Sea of Windless Storm where the blue waves like snow-clad hills roll silently out of Unlight to the long strand, bearing the white ships that return from battles on the Dark Marches of which men know nothing. He saw a great ship cast high upon the land, and the waters fell back in foam without a sound. The elven mariners were tall and terrible; their swords shone and their spears glinted and a piercing light was in their eyes. Suddenly they lifted up their voices in a song of triumph, and his heart was shaken with fear, and he fell upon his face, and they passed over him and went away into the echoing hills.

Afterwards he went no more to that strand, believing

that he was in an island realm beleaguered by the Sea, and he turned his mind towards the mountains, desiring to come to the heart of the kingdom. Once in these wanderings he was overtaken by a grey mist and strayed long at a loss, until the mist rolled away and he found that he was in a wide plain. Far off there was a great hill of shadow, and out of that shadow, which was its root, he saw the King's Tree springing up, tower upon tower, into the sky, and its light was like the sun at noon; and it bore at once leaves and flowers and fruits uncounted, and not one was the same as any other that grew on the Tree.

He never saw that Tree again, though he often sought for it. On one such journey climbing into the Outer Mountains he came to a deep dale among them, and at its bottom lay a lake, calm and unruffled though a breeze stirred the woods that surrounded it. In that dale the light was like a red sunset, but the light came up from the lake. From a low cliff that overhung it he looked down, and it seemed that he could see to an immeasurable depth; and there he beheld strange shapes of flame bending and branching and wavering like great weeds in a sea-dingle, and fiery creatures went to and fro among them. Filled with wonder he went down to the water's edge and tried it with his foot, but it was not water: it was harder than stone and sleeker than glass. He stepped on it and he fell heavily, and a ringing boom ran across the lake and echoed in its shores.

At once the breeze rose to a wild Wind, roaring like a great beast, and it swept him up and flung him on the shore, and it drove him up the slopes whirling and falling like a dead leaf. He put his arms about the stem of a young birch and clung to it, and the Wind wrestled fiercely with them, trying to tear him away; but the birch was bent down to the ground by the blast and enclosed him in its branches. When at last the Wind passed on he rose and saw that the birch was naked. It was stripped of every leaf, and it wept, and tears fell from its branches like rain. He set his hand upon its white bark, saying: 'Blessed be the birch! What can I do to make amends or give thanks?' He felt the answer of the tree pass up from his hand: 'Nothing', it said. 'Go away! The Wind is hunting you. You do not belong here. Go away and never return!'

As he climbed back out of that dale he felt the tears of the birch trickle down his face and they were bitter on his lips. His heart was saddened as he went on his long road, and for some time he did not enter Faery again. But he could not forsake it, and when he returned his desire was still stronger to go deep into the land.

At last he found a road through the Outer Mountains, and he went on till he came to the Inner Mountains, and they were high and sheer and daunting. Yet in the end he found a pass that he could scale, and upon a day

of days greatly daring he came through a narrow cleft and looked down, though he did not know it, into the Vale of Evermorn where the green surpasses the green of the meads of Outer Faery as they surpass ours in our springtime. There the air is so lucid that eyes can see the red tongues of birds as they sing on the trees upon the far side of the valley, though that is very wide and the birds are no greater than wrens.

On the inner side the mountains went down in long slopes filled with the sound of bubbling waterfalls, and in great delight he hastened on. As he set foot upon the grass of the Vale he heard elven voices singing, and on a lawn beside a river bright with lilies he came upon many maidens dancing. The speed and the grace and the ever-changing modes of their movements enchanted him, and he stepped forward towards their ring. Then suddenly they stood still, and a young maiden with flowing hair and kilted skirt came out to meet him.

She laughed as she spoke to him, saying: 'You are becoming bold, Starbrow, are you not? Have you no fear what the Queen might say, if she knew of this? Unless you have her leave'. He was abashed, for he became aware of his own thought and knew that she read it: that the star on his forehead was a passport to go wherever he wished; and now he knew that it was not. But she smiled as she spoke again: 'Come! Now that you are here you shall dance with me'; and she took his hand and led him into the ring.

There they danced together, and for a while he

knew what it was to have the swiftness and the power and the joy to accompany her. For a while. But soon as it seemed they halted again, and she stooped and took up a white flower from before her feet, and she set it in his hair. 'Farewell now!' she said. 'Maybe we shall meet again, by the Queen's leave'.

He remembered nothing of the journey home from that meeting, until he found himself riding along the roads in his own country; and in some villages people stared at him in wonder and watched him till he rode out of sight. When he came to his own house his daughter ran out and greeted him with delight—he had returned sooner than was expected, but none too soon for those that awaited him. 'Daddy!' she cried. 'Where have you been? Your star is shining bright!'

When he crossed the threshold the star dimmed again; but Nell took him by the hand and led him to the hearth, and there she turned and looked at him. 'Dear Man', she said, 'where have you been and what have you seen? There is a flower in your hair'. She lifted it gently from his head, and it lay on her hand. It seemed like a thing seen from a great distance, yet there it was, and a light came from it that cast shadows on the walls of the room, now growing dark in the evening. The shadow of the man before her loomed up and its great head was bowed over her. 'You look like a giant, Dad', said his son, who had not spoken before.

The flower did not wither nor grow dim; and they kept it as a secret and a treasure. The smith made a little casket with a key for it, and there it lay and was handed down for many generations in his kin; and those who inherited the key would at times open the casket and look long at the Living Flower, till the casket closed again: the time of its shutting was not theirs to choose.

The years did not halt in the village. Many now had passed. At the Children's Feast when he received the star the smith was not yet ten years old. Then came another Twenty-four Feast, by which time Alf had become Master Cook and had chosen a new apprentice, Harper. Twelve years later the smith had returned with the Living Flower; and now another Children's Twenty-four Feast was due in the winter to come. One day in that year Smith was walking in the woods of Outer Faery, and it was autumn. Golden leaves were on the boughs and red leaves were on the ground. Footsteps came behind him, but he did not heed them or turn round, for he was deep in thought.

On that visit he had received a summons and had made a far journey. Longer it seemed to him than any he had yet made. He was guided and guarded, but he had little memory of the ways that he had taken; for often he had been blindfolded by mist or by shadow, until at last he came to a high place under a night-sky of innumerable stars. There he was brought before the

Queen herself. She wore no crown and had no throne. She stood there in her majesty and her glory, and all about her was a great host shimmering and glittering like the stars above; but she was taller than the points of their great spears, and upon her head there burned a white flame. She made a sign for him to approach, and trembling he stepped forward. A high clear trumpet sounded, and behold! they were alone.

He stood before her, and he did not kneel in courtesy, for he was dismayed and felt that for one so lowly all gestures were in vain. At length he looked up and beheld her face and her eyes bent gravely upon him; and he was troubled and amazed, for in that moment he knew her again: the fair maid of the Green Vale, the dancer at whose feet the flowers sprang. She smiled seeing his memory, and drew towards him; and they spoke long together, for the most part without words, and he learned many things in her thought, some of which gave him joy, and others filled him with grief. Then his mind turned back retracing his life, until he came to the day of the Children's Feast and the coming of the star, and suddenly he saw again the little dancing figure with its wand, and in shame he lowered his eyes from the Queen's beauty.

But she laughed again as she had laughed in the Vale of Evermorn. 'Do not be grieved for me, Starbrow', she said. 'Nor too much ashamed of your own folk. Better a little doll, maybe, than no memory of Faery at all. For some the only glimpse. For some the awaking. Ever since that day you have desired in your heart to see me, and I have granted your wish. But I can give you no more. Now at farewell I will make you my messenger. If you meet the King, say to him: *The time has come. Let him choose*'.

'But Lady of Faery', he stammered, 'where then is the King?' For he had asked this question many times of the people of Faery, and they had all said the same: 'He has not told us'.

And the Queen answered: 'If he has not told you, Starbrow, then I may not. But he makes many journeys and may be met in unlikely places. Now kneel of your courtesy'.

Then he knelt, and she stooped and laid her hand on his head, and a great stillness came upon him; and he seemed to be both in the World and in Faery, and also outside them and surveying them, so that he was at once in bereavement, and in ownership, and in peace. When after a while the stillness passed he raised his head and stood up. The dawn was in the sky and the stars were pale, and the Queen was gone. Far off he heard the echo of a trumpet in the mountains. The high field where he stood was silent and empty: and he knew that his way now led back to bereavement.

That meeting-place was now far behind him, and here he was, walking among the fallen leaves, pondering all that he had seen and learned. The footsteps came nearer. Then suddenly a voice said at his side: 'Are you going my way, Starbrow?'

He started and came out of his thoughts, and he saw a man beside him. He was tall, and he walked lightly and quickly; he was dressed all in dark green and wore a hood that partly overshadowed his face. The smith was puzzled, for only the people of Faery called him 'Starbrow', but he could not remember ever having seen this man there before; and yet he felt uneasily that he should know him. 'What way are you going then?' he said.

'I am going back to your village now', the man answered, 'and I hope that you are also returning'.

'I am indeed', said the smith. 'Let us walk together. But now something has come back to my mind. Before I began my homeward journey a Great Lady gave me a message, but we shall soon be passing from Faery, and I do not think that I shall ever return. Will you?'

'Yes, I shall. You may give the message to me'.

'But the message was to the King. Do you know where to find him?'

'I do. What was the message?'

'The Lady only asked me to say to him: *The time has come. Let him choose*'.

'I understand. Trouble yourself no further'.

They went on then side by side in silence save for the rustle of the leaves about their feet; but after a few miles while they were still within the bounds of Faery the man halted. He turned towards the smith and threw back his hood. Then the smith knew him. He was Alf the Prentice, as the smith still called him in his own mind, remembering always the day when as a youth Alf had stood in the Hall, holding the bright knife for the cutting of the Cake, and his eyes had gleamed in the light of the candles. He must be an old man now, for he had been Master Cook for many years; but here standing under the eaves of the Outer Wood he looked like the apprentice of long ago, though more masterly: there was no grey in his hair nor line on his face, and his eyes gleamed as if they reflected a light.

'I should like to speak to you, Smith Smithson, before we go back to your country', he said. The smith wondered at that, for he himself had often wished to talk to Alf, but had never been able to do so. Alf had always greeted him kindly and had looked at him with friendly eyes, but had seemed to avoid talking to him alone. He was looking now at the smith with friendly eyes; but he lifted his hand and with his forefinger touched the star on his brow. The gleam left his eyes, and then the smith knew that it had come from the star, and that it must have been shining brightly but now was dimmed. He was surprised and drew away angrily.

'Do you not think, Master Smith', said Alf, 'that it is time for you to give this thing up?'

'What is that to you, Master Cook?' he answered. 'And why should I do so? Isn't it mine? It came to me, and may a man not keep things that come to him so, at the least as a remembrance?'

'Some things. Those that are free gifts and given for remembrance. But others are not so given. They cannot belong to a man for ever, nor be treasured as heirlooms. They are lent. You have not thought, perhaps, that someone else may need this thing. But it is so. Time is pressing'.

Then the smith was troubled, for he was a generous man, and he remembered with gratitude all that the star had brought to him. 'Then what should I do?' he asked. 'Should I give it to one of the Great in Faery? Should I give it to the King?' And as he said this a hope sprang in his heart that on such an errand he might once more enter Faery.

'You could give it to me', said Alf, 'but you might find that too hard. Will you come with me to my store-room and put it back in the box where your grandfather laid it?'

'I did not know that', said the smith.

'No one knew but me. I was the only one with him'.

'Then I suppose that you know how he came by the star, and why he put it in the box?'

'He brought it from Faery: that you know without asking', Alf answered. 'He left it behind in the hope that it might come to you, his only grandchild. So he told me, for he thought that I could arrange that. He was your mother's father. I do not know whether she told you much about him, if indeed she knew much to tell. Rider was his name, and he was a great traveller: he had seen many things and could do many things

before he settled down and become Master Cook. But he went away when you were only two years old—and they could find no one better to follow him than Nokes, poor man. Still, as we expected, I became Master in time. This year I shall make another Great Cake: the only Cook, as far as is remembered, ever to make a second one. I wish to put the star in it'.

'Very well, you shall have it', said the smith. He looked at Alf as if he was trying to read his thought. 'Do you know who will find it?'

'What is that to you, Master Smith?'

'I should like to know, if you do, Master Cook. It might make it easier for me to part with a thing so dear to me. My daughter's child is too young'.

'It might and it might not. We shall see', said Alf.

They said no more, and they went on their way until they passed out of Faery and came back at last to the village. Then they walked to the Hall; and in the world the sun was now setting and a red light was in the windows. The gilded carvings on the great door glowed, and strange faces of many colours looked down from the water-spouts under the roof. Not long ago the Hall had been re-glazed and re-painted, and there had been much debate on the Council about it. Some disliked it and called it 'new-fangled', but some with more knowledge knew that it was a return to old custom. Still, since it had cost no one a penny and the Master Cook must have paid for it himself, he was allowed to have his own way. But the smith had not seen it in such a light before, and he stood and looked at the Hall in wonder, forgetting his errand.

He felt a touch on his arm, and Alf led him round to a small door at the back. He opened it and led the smith down a dark passage into the store-room. There he lit a tall candle, and unlocking a cupboard he took down from a shelf the black box. It was polished now and adorned with silver scrolls.

He raised the lid and showed it to the smith. One small compartment was empty; the others were now filled with spices, fresh and pungent, and the smith's eyes began to water. He put his hand to his forehead, and the star came away readily, but he felt a sudden stab of pain, and tears ran down his face. Though the star shone brightly again as it lay in his hand, he could not see it, except as a blurred dazzle of light that seemed far away.

'I cannot see clearly', he said. 'You must put it in for me'. He held out his hand, and Alf took the star and laid it in its place, and it went dark.

The smith turned away without another word and groped his way to the door. On the threshold he found that his sight had cleared again. It was evening and the Even-star was shining in a luminous sky close to the Moon. As he stood for a moment looking at their beauty, he felt a hand on his shoulder and turned.

'You gave me the star freely', said Alf. 'If you still wish to know to which child it will go, I will tell you'.

'I do indeed'.

'It shall go to any one that you appoint'.

The smith was taken aback and did not answer at once. 'Well', he said hesitating, 'I wonder what you may think of my choice. I believe you have little reason to love the name of Nokes, but, well, his little great-grandson, Nokes of Townsend's Tim, is coming to the Feast. Nokes of Townsend is quite different'.

'I have observed that', said Alf. 'He had a wise mother'.

'Yes, my Nell's sister. But apart from the kinship I love little Tim. Though he's not an obvious choice'.

Alf smiled. 'Neither were you', he said. 'But I agree. Indeed I had already chosen Tim'.

'Then why did you ask me to choose?'

'The Queen wished me to do so. If you had chosen differently I should have given way'.

The smith looked long at Alf. Then suddenly he bowed low. 'I understand at last, sir', he said. 'You have done us too much honour'.

'I have been repaid', said Alf. 'Go home now in peace !'

When the smith reached his own house on the western outskirts of the village he found his son by the door of the forge. He had just locked it, for the day's work was done, and now he stood looking up the white road by which his father used to return from his journeys. Hearing footsteps, he turned in surprise to see him coming from the village, and he ran forward to meet him. He put his arms about him in loving welcome.

'I've been hoping for you since yesterday, Dad', he said. Then looking into his father's face he said anxiously: 'How tired you look! You have walked far, maybe?'

'Very far indeed, my son. All the way from Daybreak to Evening'.

They went into the house together, and it was dark except for the fire flickering on the hearth. His son lit candles, and for a while they sat by the fire without speaking; for a great weariness and bereavement was on the smith. At last he looked round, as if coming to himself, and he said: 'Why are we alone?'

His son looked hard at him. 'Why? Mother's over at Minor, at Nan's. It's the little lad's second birthday. They hoped you would be there too'.

'Ah yes. I ought to have been. I should have been, Ned, but I was delayed; and I have had matters to think of that put all else out of mind for a time. But I did not forget Tomling'.

He put his hand in his breast and drew out a little wallet of soft leather. 'I have brought him something. A trinket old Nokes maybe would call it—but it comes out of Faery, Ned'. Out of the wallet he took a little thing of silver. It was like the smooth stem of a tiny lily from the top of which came three delicate flowers, bending down like shapely bells. And bells they were, for when he shook them gently each flower rang with a small clear note. At the sweet sound the candles flickered and then for a moment shone with a white light.

Ned's eyes were wide with wonder. 'May I look at it, Dad?' he said. He took it with careful fingers and peered into the flowers. 'The work is a marvel!' he said. 'And, Dad, there is a scent in the bells: a scent that reminds me of, reminds me, well of something I've forgotten'.

'Yes, the scent comes for a little while after the bells have rung. But don't fear to handle it, Ned. It was made for a babe to play with. He can do it no harm, and he'll take none from it'.

The smith put the gift back in the wallet and stowed it away. 'I'll take it over to Wootton Minor myself tomorrow', he said. 'Nan and her Tom, and Mother, will forgive me, maybe. As for Tomling, his time has not come yet for the counting of days . . . and of weeks, and of months, and of years'.

'That's right. You go, Dad. I'd be glad to go with you; but it will be some time before I can get over to Minor. I couldn't have gone today, even if I hadn't waited here for you. There's a lot of work in hand, and more coming in'.

'No, no, Smith's son! Make it a holiday! The name of grandfather hasn't weakened my arms yet a while. Let the work come! There'll be two pairs of hands to tackle it now, all working days. I shall not be going on journeys again, Ned: not on long ones, if you understand me'.

'It's that way is it, Dad? I wondered what had become of the star. That's hard'. He took his father's hand. 'I'm grieved for you; but there's good in it too, for this house. Do you know, Master Smith, there is much you can teach me yet, if you have the time. And I do not mean only the working of iron'.

They had supper together, and long after they had finished they still sat at the table, while the smith told his son of his last journey in Faery, and of other things that came to his mind—but about the choice of the next holder of the star he said nothing.

At last his son looked at him, and 'Father', he said, 'do you remember the day when you came back with the Flower? And I said that you looked like a giant by your shadow. The shadow was the truth. So it was the Queen herself that you danced with. Yet you have given up the star. I hope it may go to someone as worthy. The child should be grateful'.

'The child won't know', said the smith. 'That's the way with such gifts. Well, there it is. I have handed it on and come back to hammer and tongs'.

It is a strange thing, but old Nokes, who had scoffed at his apprentice, had never been able to put out of his mind the disappearance of the star in the Cake, although that event had happened so many years ago.

He had grown fat and lazy, and retired from his office when he was sixty (no great age in the village). He was now near the end of his eighties, and was of enormous bulk, for he still ate heavily and doted on sugar. Most of his days, when not at table, he spent in a big chair by the window of his cottage, or by the door if it was fine weather. He liked talking, since he still had many opinions to air; but lately his talk mostly turned to the one Great Cake that he had made (as he was now firmly convinced), for whenever he fell asleep it came into his dreams. Prentice sometimes stopped for a word or two. So the old cook still called him, and he expected himself to be called Master. That Prentice was careful to do; which was a point in his favour, though there were others that Nokes was more fond of.

One afternoon Nokes was nodding in his chair by the door after his dinner. He woke with a start to find Prentice standing by and looking down at him. 'Hullo!' he said. 'I'm glad to see you, for that cake's been on my mind again. I was thinking of it just now in fact. It was the best cake I ever made, and that's saying something. But perhaps you have forgotten it'.

'No, Master. I remember it very well. But what is troubling you? It was a good cake, and it was enjoyed and praised'.

'Of course. I made it. But that doesn't trouble me. It's the little trinket, the star. I cannot make up my mind what became of it. Of course it wouldn't melt. I only said that to stop the children from being frightened. I have wondered if one of them did not swallow it. But is that likely? You might swallow one of those little coins and not notice it, but not that star. It was small but it had sharp points'.

'Yes, Master. But do you really know what the star was made of? Don't trouble your mind about it. Someone swallowed it, I assure you'.

'Then who? Well, I've a long memory, and that day sticks in it somehow. I can recall all the children's names. Let me think. It must have been Miller's Molly! She was greedy and bolted her food. She's as fat as a sack now'.

'Yes, there are some folk who get like that, Master. But Molly did not bolt her cake. She found two trinkets in her slice'.

'Oh, did she? Well, it was Cooper's Harry then. A barrel of a boy with a big mouth like a frog's'.

'I should have said, Master, that he was a nice boy with a large friendly grin. Anyway he was so careful that he took his slice to pieces before he ate it. He found nothing but cake'.

'Then it must have been that little pale girl, Draper's Lily. She used to swallow pins as a baby and came to no harm'.

'Not Lily, Master. She only ate the paste and the sugar, and gave the inside to the boy that sat next to her'.

'Then I give up. Who was it? You seem to have been watching very closely. If you're not making it all up'.

'It was the Smith's son, Master; and I think it was good for him'.

'Go on!' laughed old Nokes. 'I ought to have known you were having a game with me. Don't be ridiculous! Smith was a quiet slow boy then. He makes more noise now: a bit of a songster, I hear; but he's cautious. No risks for him. Chews twice before he swallows, and always did, if you take my meaning'.

'I do, Master. Well, if you won't believe it was Smith, I can't help you. Perhaps it doesn't matter much now. Will it ease your mind if I tell you that the star is back in the box now? Here it is!'

Prentice was wearing a dark green cloak, which Nokes now noticed for the first time. From its folds he produced the black box and opened it under the old cook's nose. 'There is the star, Master, down in the corner'.

Old Nokes began coughing and sneezing, but at last he looked into the box. 'So it is!' he said. 'At least it looks like it'.

'It is the same one, Master. I put it there myself a few days ago. It will go back in the Great Cake this winter'.

'A-ha!' said Nokes, leering at Prentice; and then he laughed till he shook like a jelly. 'I see, I see! Twenty-four children and twenty-four lucky bits, and the star was one extra. So you nipped it out before the baking and kept it for another time. You were always a tricky fellow: nimble one might say. And thrifty: wouldn't waste a bee's knee of butter. Ha, ha, ha! So that was the way of it. I might have guessed. Well, that's cleared up. Now I can have a nap in peace'. He settled down in his chair. 'Mind that prentice-man of yours plays you no tricks! The artful don't know all the arts, they say'. He closed his eyes.

"Godbye, Master!' said Prentice, shutting the box with such a snap that the cook opened his eyes again. 'Nokes', he said, 'your knowledge is so great that I have only twice ventured to tell you anything. I told you that the star came from Faery; and I have told you that it went to the smith. You laughed at me. Now at parting I will tell you one thing more. Don't laugh again! You are a vain old fraud, fat, idle and sly. I did most of your work. Without thanks you learned all that you could from me—except respect for Faery, and a little courtesy. You have not even enough to bid me good day'.

'If it comes to courtesy', said Nokes, 'I see none in calling your elders and betters by ill names. Take your Fairy and your nonsense somewhere else! Good day to you, if that's what you're waiting for. Now go along with you!' He flapped his hand mockingly. 'If you've got one of your fairy friends hidden in the Kitchen, send him to me and I'll have a look at him. If he waves his little wand and makes me thin again, I'll think better of him', he laughed.

'Would you spare a few moments for the King of Faery?' the other answered. To Nokes's dismay he grew taller as he spoke. He threw back his cloak. He was dressed like a Master Cook at a Feast, but his white garments shimmered and glinted, and on his forehead was a great jewel like a radiant star. His face was young but stern.

'Old man', he said, 'you are at least not my elder. As to my better: you have often sneered at me behind my back. Do you challenge me now openly?' He stepped forward, and Nokes shrank from him, trembling. He tried to shout for help but found that he could hardly whisper.

'No, sir!' he croaked. 'Don't do me a harm! I'm only a poor old man'.

The King's face softened. 'Alas, yes! You speak the truth. Do not be afraid! Be at ease! But will you not expect the King of Faery to do something for you before he leaves you? I grant you your wish. Farewell! Now go to sleep!'

He wrapped his cloak about him again and went away towards the Hall; but before he was out of sight the old cook's goggling eyes had shut and he was snoring.

When the old cook woke again the sun was going down. He rubbed his eyes and shivered a little, for the autumn air was chilly. 'Ugh! What a dream!' he said. 'It must have been that pork at dinner'.

From that day he became so afraid of having more bad dreams of that sort that he hardly dared eat anything for fear that it might upset him, and his meals became very short and plain. He soon became lean, and his clothes and his skin hung on him in folds and creases. The children called him old Rag-and-Bones. Then for a time he found that he could get about the village again and walk with no more help than a stick; and he lived many years longer than he would otherwise have done. Indeed it is said that he just made his century: the only memorable thing he ever achieved. But till his last year he could be heard saying to any that would listen to his tale: 'Alarming, you might call it; but a silly dream, when you come to think of it. King o' Fairy! Why, he hadn't no wand. And if you stop eating you grow thinner. That's natural. Stands to reason. There ain't no magic in it'.

The time for the Twenty-four Feast came round. Smith was there to sing songs and his wife to help with the children. Smith looked at them as they sang and danced, and he thought that they were more beautiful and lively than they had been in his boyhood—for a moment it crossed his mind to wonder what Alf might have been doing in his spare time. Any one of them seemed fit to find the stair. But his eyes were mostly on Tim: a rather plump little boy, clumsy in the dances, but with a sweet voice in the singing. At table he sat silent watching the sharpening of the knife and the cutting of the Cake. Suddenly, he piped up: 'Dear Mr. Cook, only cut me a small slice please. I've eaten so much already, I feel rather full'.

'All right, Tim', said Alf. 'I'll cut you a special slice. I think you'll find it go down easily'.

Smith watched as Tim ate his cake slowly, but with evident pleasure; though when he found no trinket or coin in it he looked disappointed. But soon a light began to shine in his eyes, and he laughed and became merry, and sang softly to himself. Then he got up and began to dance all alone with an odd grace that he had never shown before. The children all laughed and clapped.

'All is well then', thought Smith. 'So you are my heir. I wonder what strange places the star will lead you to? Poor old Nokes. Still I suppose he will never know what a shocking thing has happened in his family'.

He never did. But one thing happened at that Feast that pleased him mightily. Before it was over the Master Cook took leave of the children and of all the others that were present.

'I will say goodbye now', he said. 'In a day or two I shall be going away. Master Harper is quite ready to take over. He is a very good cook, and as you know he comes from your own village. I shall go back home. I do not think you will miss me'.

The children said goodbye cheerfully, and thanked the Cook prettily for his beautiful Cake. Only little Tim took his hand and said quietly, 'I'm sorry'.

In the village there were in fact several families that did miss Alf for some time. A few of his friends, especially Smith and Harper, grieved at his going, and they kept the Hall gilded and painted in memory of Alf. Most people, however, were content. They had had him for a very long time and were not sorry to have a change. But old Nokes thumped his stick on the floor and said roundly: 'He's gone at last! And I'm glad for one. I never liked him. He was artful. Too nimble, you might say'.